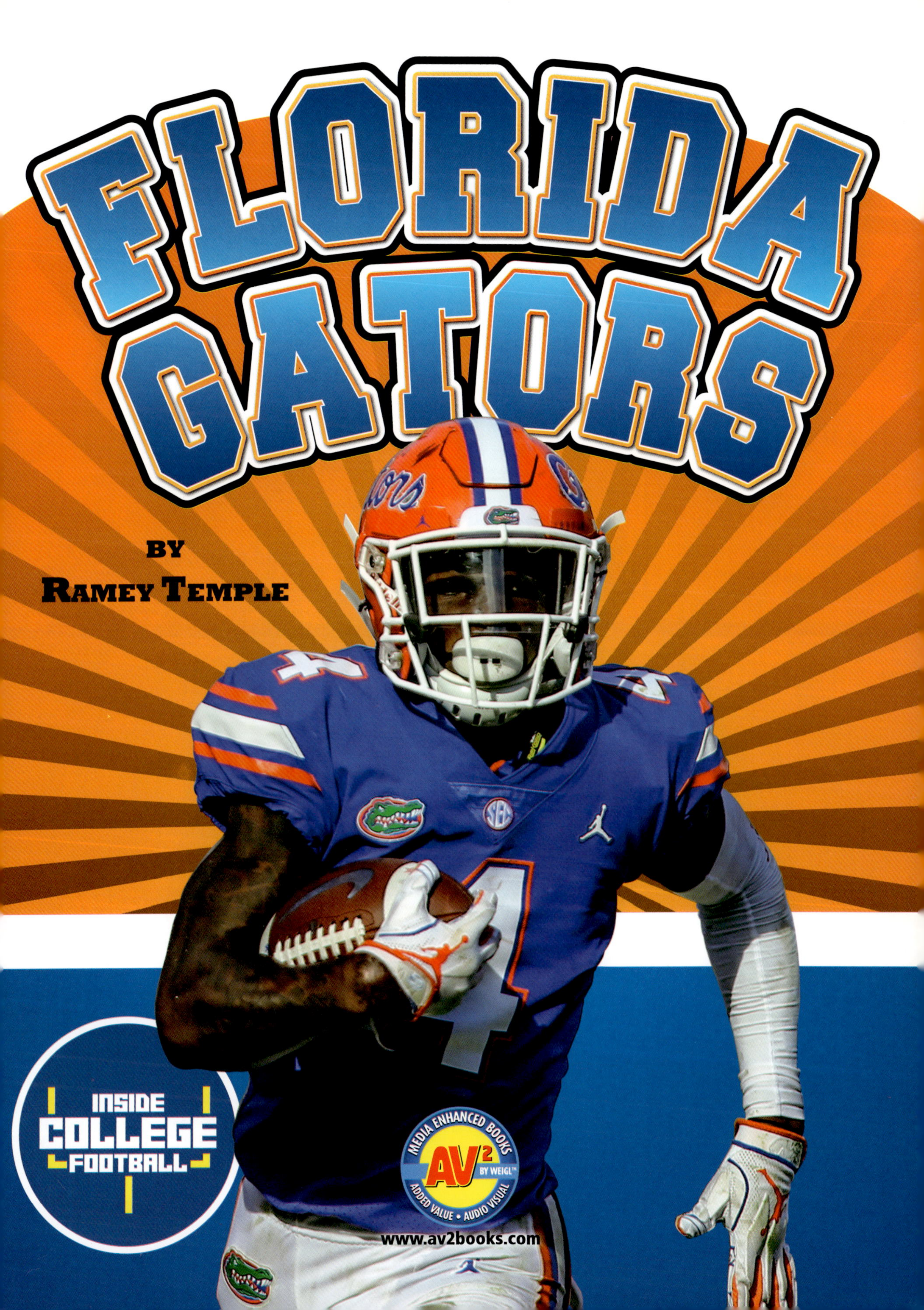
FLORIDA GATORS
BY
RAMEY TEMPLE
INSIDE
COLLEGE
FOOTBALL
MEDIA ENHANCED BOOKS
AV2
BY WEIGL
ADDED VALUE • AUDIO VISUAL
www.av2books.com

Go to www.av2books.com, and enter this book's unique code.

BOOK CODE

AVA49683

AV² by Weigl brings you media enhanced books that support active learning.

AV² provides enriched content that supplements and complements this book. Weigl's AV² books strive to create inspired learning and engage young minds in a total learning experience.

Your AV² Media Enhanced books come alive with...

Audio
Listen to sections of the book read aloud.

Video
Watch informative video clips.

Embedded Weblinks
Gain additional information for research.

Try This!
Complete activities and hands-on experiments.

Key Words
Study vocabulary, and complete a matching word activity.

Quizzes
Test your knowledge.

Slideshow
View images and captions, and prepare a presentation.

... and much, much more!

Published by AV² by Weigl
350 5th Avenue, 59th Floor
New York, NY 10118
Website: www.av2books.com

Library of Congress Control Number: 2018968221

ISBN 978-1-7911-0111-4 (hardcover)
ISBN 978-1-7911-0112-1 (multi-user eBook)
ISBN 978-1-7911-0113-8 (single-user eBook)

Printed in Guangzhou, China
1 2 3 4 5 6 7 8 9 0 23 22 21 20 19

042019
102318

Project Coordinator: Jared Siemens Designer: Terry Paulhus

Every reasonable effort has been made to trace ownership and to obtain permission to reprint copyright material. The publishers would be pleased to have any errors or omissions brought to their attention so that they may be corrected in subsequent printings.

The publisher acknowledges Alamy, Getty Images, Newscom, and Wikimedia Commons as its primary image suppliers for this title.

Florida Gators

CONTENTS

Introduction

The University of Florida (UF) football team is known as the Gators. Part of the storied Southeastern Conference (SEC), they have played in more than 40 bowl games and won multiple National Championships. Florida fans are known as Gator Nation. The Gators host their opponents at Ben Hill Griffin Stadium, nicknamed "The Swamp."

The Gators have many entertaining traditions. Between the third and fourth quarter of every game, fans stand up, lock arms, and sway while singing a song called "We are the Boys." The "Gator Chomp" is one of the most **iconic** fan traditions. When the band plays the *Jaws* theme song throughout the game, fans simulate alligator jaws snapping by quickly opening and closing their outstretched arms. They also do the Gator Chomp before every kickoff and after big plays throughout the game. There is also a tradition where someone leads the "Two Bits" chant at the beginning of each home game. The chant goes, "Two-bits. Four-bits. Six-bits. A dollar. All the Gators, stand up and holler."

After an injury ended his 2016 season in the first week of play, Dre Massey returned to the field the following year and logged 11 catches for 149 yards for the Gators.

Running back Lamical Perine scored three touchdowns in a 2018 game against the Vanderbilt University Commodores, becoming the first UF running back to score three touchdowns in a single game since 2005.

Gators

FLORIDA

Stadium Steve Spurrier–Florida Field at Ben Hill Griffin Stadium

Division Southeastern Conference (SEC) Eastern

Head Coach Dan Mullen

Location Gainesville, Florida

National Championships 3

Nicknames The Gators, UF

27 Head Coaches

9 Conference Championships

3 Heisman Memorial Trophy Winners

44 Bowl Games Played

History

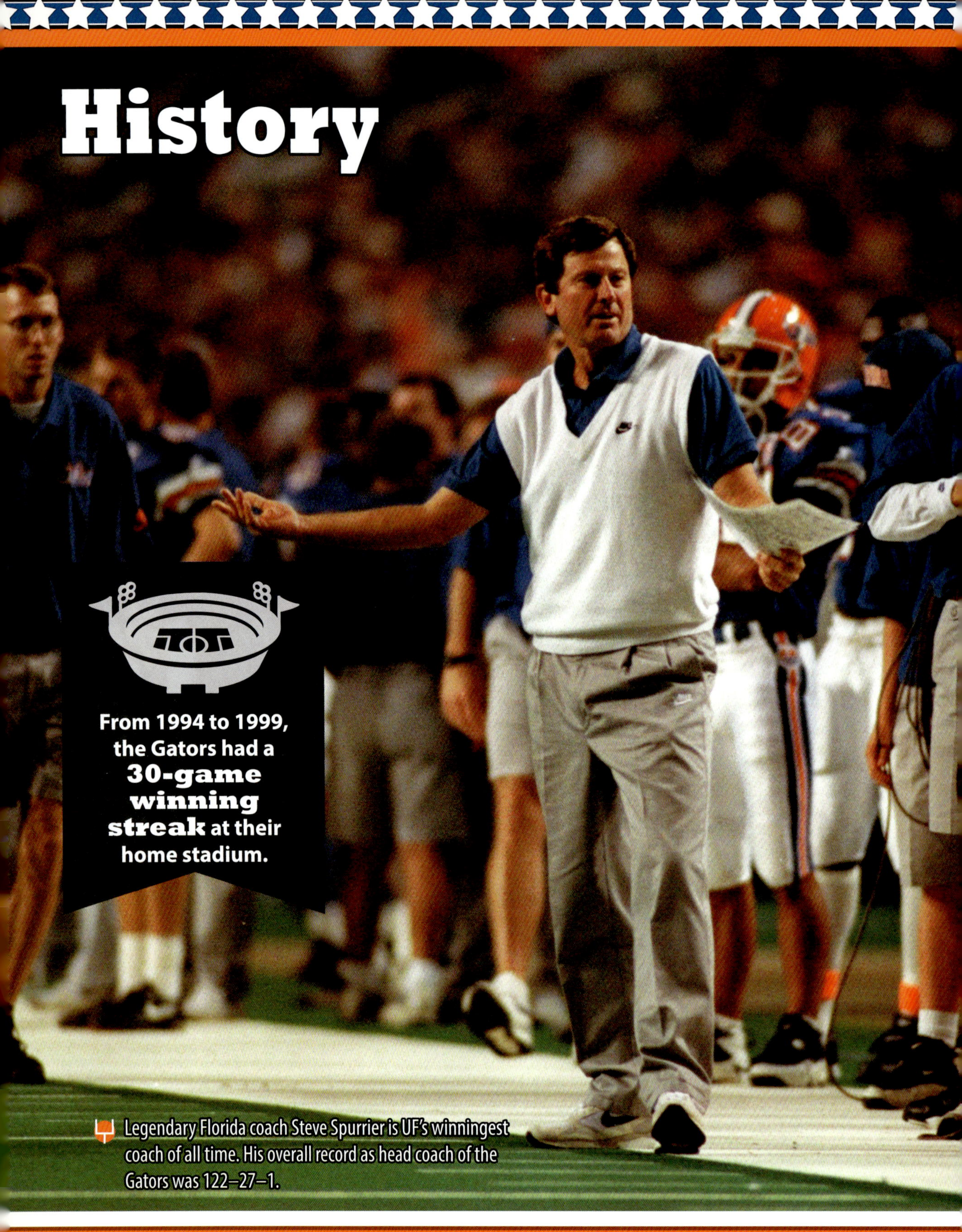

From 1994 to 1999, the Gators had a **30-game winning streak** at their home stadium.

Legendary Florida coach Steve Spurrier is UF's winningest coach of all time. His overall record as head coach of the Gators was 122–27–1.

The University of Florida fielded its first football team in 1906. The team played in its first **postseason** game in 1912 in the Bacardi Bowl, an exhibition game in Cuba. Three decades later, the 1960s brought winning head coach Ray Graves to the team. In 1966, starting quarterback Steve Spurrier won the Gators' first Heisman Memorial Trophy.

Spurrier took over as head coach in 1989. The '90s were a great decade for the Gators. They won their first SEC title in 1991. With Spurrier as their coach, they won four more SEC titles in a row from 1993 to 1996. The Gators also won their very first National Championship in 1996 by crushing Florida State University 52–20 in the Nokia Sugar Bowl. Also in 1996, quarterback Danny Wuerffel became the second Gator to win the Heisman Trophy.

Urban Meyer took over as head coach in 2005, leading the Gators to an impressive two National Championships in three years. During that time, star quarterback Tim Tebow won the school's third Heisman. The University of Florida hired Coach Dan Mullen after the Gators' 2017 losing season.

The 1911 Gators are the only undefeated team in UF history. The Gator officially became the UF mascot in 1911. Some fans believe team captain Neal "Bo Gator" Storter was behind this decision.

The Stadium

Before the upper seating decks were added, the original Florida Field seated fewer than 22,000 fans. Today, about 90,000 people can gather in the stadium to watch the Gators play.

The Gators originally played football at Fleming Field. Florida Field was built in 1930 and named in honor of Florida service members who had lost their lives in World War I (1914–1918). The stadium was renamed in 1989 to Ben Hill Griffin Stadium at Florida Field, in honor of a generous Gator supporter. In 2016, the stadium was renamed yet again to Steve Spurrier–Florida Field at Ben Hill Griffin Stadium.

Ever since the 1990s, the Gators' stadium has been nicknamed "The Swamp." Steve Spurrier gave the stadium its nickname. He said swamps were hot, humid places where gators felt at home, but where their enemies felt uncomfortable. The stadium is known for being one of the toughest stadiums for visiting teams to play.

The Swamp has had many upgrades over the years. In 1950 and 1965, there were expansions to increase seating capacity. South end zone seats, an athletic training center, and a press box were added in 1982. In 2007, the stadium underwent a $28-million **renovation**, including an expansion of the exercise room and football offices. Between 2010 and 2017, a new LED ribbon board was added, two large video boards were installed in the end zones, and the **synthetic** playing surface was replaced with natural grass.

"The Swamp" is more than just a nickname. The stadium was built in a ravine where natural groundwater caused the area to become a muddy pit. Today, large underground pipes redirect the water to a nearby pond.

Where They Play

Welcome to Steve Spurrier–Florida Field at Ben Hill Griffin Stadium, home of the Florida Gators. Nearly 90,000 fans gather on game days to do the Gator Chomp and cheer for the boys in blue and orange. Players, UF alumni, and Gators fans love calling The Swamp home.

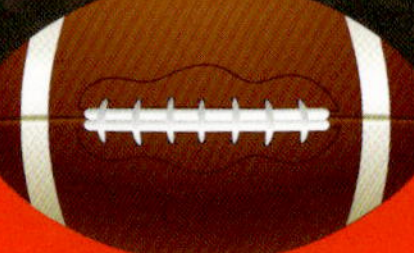

SEC WEST

1. **Auburn University**
   Auburn, Alabama
2. **Louisiana State University**
   Baton Rouge, Louisiana
3. **Mississippi State University**
   Starkville, Mississippi
4. **Texas A&M University**
   College Station, Texas
5. **University of Alabama**
   Tuscaloosa, Alabama
6. **University of Arkansas**
   Fayetteville, Arkansas
7. **University of Mississippi**
   Oxford, Mississippi

Arena
Steve Spurrier–Florida Field at Ben Hill Griffin Stadium

Location
Gainesville, Florida

Broke Ground
April 16, 1930

Completed
October 27, 1930

Surface
Real Grass

Features
- Seating capacity is 88,548
- Largest football stadium in Florida
- Statues outside stadium honoring the Gators' three Heisman Trophy winners

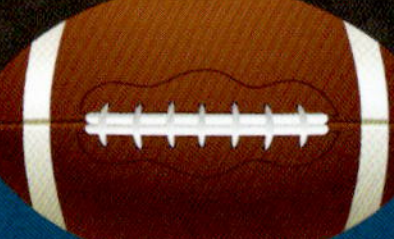

SEC EAST

1. ★ **University of Florida**
   Gainesville, Florida
2. **University of Georgia**
   Athens, Georgia
3. **University of Kentucky**
   Lexington, Kentucky
4. **University of Missouri**
   Columbia, Missouri
5. **University of South Carolina**
   Columbia, South Carolina
6. **University of Tennessee**
   Knoxville, Tennessee
7. **Vanderbilt University**
   Nashville, Tennessee

NORTH DAKOTA
SOUTH DAKOTA
NEBRASKA
KANSAS
OKLAHOMA
TEXAS
MINNESOTA
IOWA
MISSOURI
ARKANSAS
LOUISIANA
WISCONSIN
ILLINOIS
MISSISSIPPI
MICHIGAN
INDIANA
KENTUCKY
TENNESSEE
ALABAMA
OHIO
WEST VIRGINIA
VIRGINIA
NORTH CAROLINA
SOUTH CAROLINA
GEORGIA
FLORIDA
PENNSYLVANIA
NEW YORK
VERMONT
NEW HAMPSHIRE
MAINE
MASSACHUSETTS
RHODE ISLAND
CONNECTICUT
NEW JERSEY
DELAWARE
MARYLAND
WASHINGTON, D.C.
Atlantic Ocean
Gulf of Mexico
1
2
3
4
5
6
7
2
3
4
5
6
7
N
S
E
W
SCALE
0 miles
500 miles
0 kilometers
500 km
LEGEND
Home Stadium
SEC West
SEC East
United States
Other Countries
Water

The Uniforms

In a **2017** game against Texas A&M University, Gators players wore **alligator-themed** alternate uniforms. The helmets were swamp green with a Gator Head logo.

Although fans disliked them, the green Gator uniforms were designed to honor the 25th anniversary of Steve Spurrier's nickname for Ben Hill Griffin Stadium, "The Swamp."

The Gators' uniform consists of blue jerseys, white pants, and orange helmets with the word "Gators" on both sides. There have been minimal changes to the uniforms over the years. For the 2018–19 season, UF switched from Nike to the Nike-owned Jordan Brand as its new uniform provider. The uniforms look similar to past versions, but now have the brand's Jumpman **logo** where the Nike Swoosh used to be.

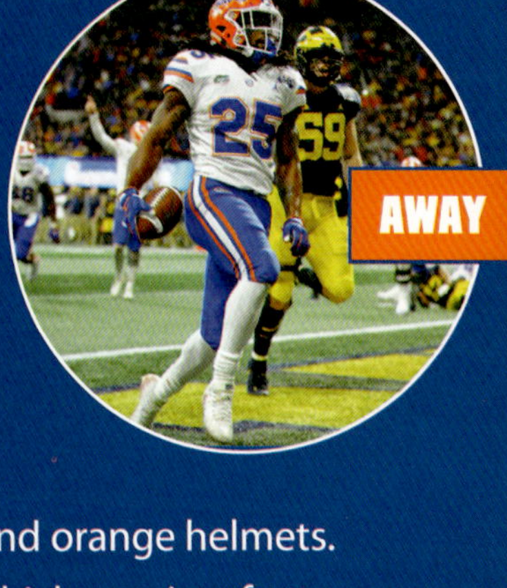

Besides their standard home uniforms, the Gators have other uniform options as well. They have their "away whites," which are worn during away games and consist of white jerseys, blue pants, and orange helmets. They also have their "orange alternates," which consist of orange jerseys, white pants, and orange helmets. The alternate uniforms are used at various times throughout the year. Whatever the combination, the Gators are sure to look sharp in blue, orange, and white.

With the exception of the swamp green alligator-themed uniform, the Gators' alternate uniforms do not look much different from their regular uniforms. The team has worn some combination of orange, blue, and white since it took the field more than 100 years ago.

Student Athletes

Freshman player Amari Burney appeared in 12 games for the Gators, and was named to the SEC Academic Honor Roll for 2018.

Being a college student athlete is hard work. Student athletes have to perform well on the football field and in the classroom. UF student athletes are required to meet a minimum grade point average and attend all of their classes. They have access to a study hall, tutoring, and mental health services through the Otis Hawkins Center. The center also provides athletes with health education and a nutrition suite where they can get healthy snacks, vitamins, and supplements. The University of Florida offers many other services to help student athletes balance football and academics.

Many student athletes are given athletic scholarships. An athletic scholarship is a financial aid agreement between the athlete and the college or university. Athletes who do not receive an athletic scholarship can also be "walk-on" members of the team. This means they are on the team, but without athletic financial aid. UF typically awards the maximum number of football scholarships allowed, which is 85.

Wide receiver Josh Hammond dominates on the field and in the classroom at the University of Florida. He is a two-time SEC Academic Honor Roll student, and during the 2018 season, he made 28 catches for 369 yards and scored four touchdowns for the Gators.

Bowl Games

During **Urban Meyer's** six seasons as head coach, the Gators went to **six bowl games.**

The Gators ended Jim McElwain's last full season as head coach at UF with a 30–3 defeat of the University of Iowa Hawkeyes in the 2017 Outback Bowl.

Bowl games are a unique sports tradition in college football. In the beginning of college football, there was no true postseason. Today, a variety of postseason bowl games are played. Bowl games give teams the opportunity to continue striving for recognition and victory after the end of regular play. There are currently 40 bowl games played in various combinations each year. These games are chosen with input from teams, sponsors, and the College Football Playoff Selection Committee. The game **matchups** are announced in December.

The Gators have played in many different bowl games, including numerous Sugar Bowls and Gator Bowls. They went to an impressive 11 bowl games under Coach Spurrier. UF has played in 44 bowls total, and its bowl record is 23–21. Most recently, the Gators won the 2018 Peach Bowl versus the University of Michigan Wolverines.

Legendary UF quarterback Tim Tebow was named the Most Valuable Player (MVP) of the 2010 Sugar Bowl, where UF defeated the University of Cincinnati Bearcats 51–24. Tebow's record-setting performance included 320 first-half passing yards, and 31 pass completions in 35 attempts.

The Coaches

When **Steve Spurrier** became head coach, he created the **Ray Graves Award**. This award is given annually to the team's MVP.

Dan Mullen finished his first season as Florida's head coach with a 10–3 overall record and a Peach Bowl victory over the University of Michigan Wolverines.

The Gators' football program has been shaped by a few notable head coaches. Ray Graves took over as head coach of the emerging program in 1960 and coached for 10 seasons. Former Gators quarterback Steve Spurrier began as head coach in 1990, leading the Gators to a very impressive 122–27–1 record. Urban Meyer was only with the Gators for six seasons, but he left a lasting mark on the program. Florida's current head coach is Dan Mullen.

RAY GRAVES Ray Graves was the second-winningest coach in UF program history. As head coach from 1960 to 1969, he led Florida to its first appearance in both the Orange Bowl and Sugar Bowl. Spurrier won the Heisman for his performance during the 1966–67 season. Graves finished his coaching job at UF with a 70–31–4 record. He was **inducted** into the College Football **Hall of Fame** in 1990.

STEVE SPURRIER Steve Spurrier went back to his alma mater to take on the role of UF head coach in 1990. He led the Gators to six SEC championships and their first-ever National Championship in 1996. He resigned after the 2001 season and coached the Washington Redskins in the National Football League (NFL) for two seasons before returning to college coaching. Spurrier was inducted into the College Football Hall of Fame for his coaching in 2017.

URBAN MEYER Urban Meyer coached the Gators from 2005 to 2010. During this time, he led the team to two SEC championships and two National Championships in 2006 and 2008. He also coached star quarterback Tim Tebow to a Heisman in 2007. Meyer's bowl record was 5–1 and his overall record was 65–15. Meyer retired from coaching in 2018 after seven seasons at Ohio State University.

The Mascot

Albert and Alberta have a variety of costumes, including their traditional orange outfits, a dressier combination for special occasions, and an all-blue outfit for the Gators' annual game against the University of Tennessee Volunteers.

Since the early 1900s, an alligator has been the symbol of the University of Florida. Beginning in 1957, a live alligator named Albert became UF's mascot. During home games, he was kept on the sidelines. There were several different live alligator mascots between 1957 and 1970.

In 1970, the school stopped using live alligators and introduced a new costumed mascot named Albert the Alligator. His sidekick, Alberta the Alligator, debuted in 1986. Albert and Alberta wear the blue and orange team colors and help stir up fan excitement from the sidelines. Sometimes, Albert also leads the "Two Bits" chant at the beginning of each home game. A bronze statue of Albert and Alberta in their game-day attire stands outside the University of Florida's Emerson Alumni Hall. The statue faces Ben Hill Griffin Stadium. Many students and fans walk past the statue on game days and touch it for good luck.

The students who portray Albert and Alberta Alligator remain anonymous, even after they have left the University of Florida. The university wants the mascots to be more about the legacy of UF than about the individuals inside the costumes.

Legends of the Past

For many players, their time with the Gators is the start of a promising football career. These are some of the best-known football players to play for the University of Florida.

Tim Tebow

During his time at UF, superstar quarterback Tim Tebow helped the Gators win two National Championships in 2006 and 2008. He won both the Heisman Trophy and the Davey O'Brien Award for outstanding quarterback in 2007. Tebow was **drafted** by the Denver Broncos in the first round of the 2010 NFL draft. He signed a five-year contract and helped lead the team to the NFL playoffs in 2011. Tebow was traded to the New York Jets in 2012. He retired from the NFL in 2015, and now appears on ESPN as a college football analyst.

Position: Quarterback
Seasons: 2006–2009 (Florida Gators), 2010–2011 (Denver Broncos), 2012 (New York Jets)
Born: August 14, 1987, Makati, Philippines

Emmitt Smith

Considered one of the SEC's best running backs of all time, Emmitt Smith played at UF for three seasons. In his rookie year, he was named National Freshman of the Year. He was also voted SEC Player of the Year in 1989. He set 58 school records, many of which remain unbroken today. Smith was drafted by the Dallas Cowboys in the first round of the 1990 draft. He won three Super Bowls with the Cowboys and was named MVP of the 1993 Super Bowl. Smith holds the NFL's career rushing touchdown record, with 164, and is one of two non-kickers in the NFL to score more than 1,000 points. He retired from football after the 2004 season.

Position: Running Back
Seasons: 1987–1989 (Florida Gators), 1990–2002 (Dallas Cowboys), 2003–2004 (Arizona Cardinals)
Born: May 15, 1969, Pensacola, Florida

Danny Wuerffel

Quarterback Danny Wuerffel was part of the Gators team that won four SEC titles in a row from 1993 to 1996. He had 114 touchdown passes while at UF, which was the most in SEC history at the time. Wuerffel was drafted in 1997 by the New Orleans Saints. He played with the Saints for three seasons. The following summer during the NFL offseason, he played with the Rhein Fire of NFL Europe. He led the Fire to the 2000 World Bowl. Wuerffel retired from the NFL in 2004 and was inducted into the College Football Hall of Fame in 2013.

Position: Quarterback
Seasons: 1993–1996 (Florida Gators), 1997–1999 (New Orleans Saints), 2000 (Rhein Fire NFL Europe), 2000 (Green Bay Packers), 2001 (Chicago Bears), 2002 (Washington Redskins)
Born: May 27, 1974, Fort Walton Beach, Florida

Jordan Reed

Jordan Reed was initially recruited to UF as a quarterback, but moved to tight end. Playing under Coach Meyer, he had 79 receptions and six touchdowns during his college career. He was drafted by the Washington Redskins in the third round of the 2013 draft. In 2015, Reed caught 87 passes and had 11 touchdowns in 14 games. He was named to the **Pro Bowl** in 2016. Reed initially signed a four-year contract with the Redskins, and in 2016 signed a five-year contract extension.

Position: Tight End
Seasons: 2010–2012 (Florida Gators), 2013–Present (Washington Redskins)
Born: July 3, 1990, New London, Connecticut

All-Time Records

482

Single-Game Passing Yards

Star quarterback Tim Tebow had 482 passing yards in a 2009 game against the University of Cincinnati Bearcats, a single-game record for UF.

316

Single-Game Rushing Yards

Powerhouse Emmitt Smith set the school record with 316 rushing yards in a game versus the University of New Mexico Lobos in 1989.

88

Single-Season Receptions

During his 1969 year, Carlos Alvarez set the University of Florida record for single-season receptions, with 88 receptions. The record has not been broken, but Chad Jackson tied it in 2005.

114

Career Passing Touchdowns

During his time at UF, quarterback Danny Wuerffel broke the school record with 114 passing touchdowns in his career.

70

Career Field Goals

Kicker Caleb Sturgis holds the Gators' record for career field goals made, with 70 from 2008 to 2012.

Timeline

Throughout the team's history, the Florida Gators have had many memorable events that have become defining moments for the team and its fans.

In 1906, the Gators football program begins.

1900 1920 1940 1960

1912
The University of Florida plays in its first unofficial postseason bowl, an exhibition game called the Bacardi Bowl in Havana, Cuba.

1930
Florida Field Stadium is built.

1949
The "Two Bits" tradition begins. At the beginning of each home game, the fans are led in the "Two Bits" chant.

1966
Steve Spurrier wins the team's first Heisman Trophy.

1970
The Albert the Alligator mascot debuts.

The Future

After a rough 2017 season, Dan Mullen was hired as the new head coach in 2018. Florida fans have high hopes for an improved team with a boosted morale under their new coaching staff. They look forward to seeing the Gators bounce back and triumph in the SEC and on the national stage.

1989
Steve Spurrier is hired as head coach.

1996
Danny Wuerffel wins the Heisman Trophy.

2006
UF wins the National Championship.

2007
Tim Tebow wins the team's third Heisman Trophy.

1980 — 2000 — 2020

In 1996, the Gators win their first National Championship.

2008
The Gators win their third National Championship.

1981
The famous Gator Chomp is introduced for the first time during a game versus the University of Maryland Tarrapins.

2018
UF wins the Peach Bowl versus the Michigan Wolverines.

Write a Biography

Life Story

A person's life story can be the subject of a book. This kind of book is called a biography. Biographies often describe the lives of people who have achieved great success. These people may be alive today, or they may have lived many years ago. Reading a biography can help you learn more about a great person.

Get the Facts

Use this book, and research in the library and on the internet, to find out more about your favorite player. Learn as much about him as you can. What position does he play? What are his statistics in important categories? Has he set any records? Also, be sure to write down key events in the person's life. What was his childhood like? What has he accomplished off the field? Is there anything else that makes this person special or unusual?

Use the Concept Web

A concept web is a useful research tool. Read the questions in the concept web on the following page. Answer the questions in your notebook. Your answers will help you write a biography.

Concept Web

Adulthood

- Where does this individual currently reside?
- Does he have a family?

Your Opinion

- What did you learn from the books you read in your research?
- Would you suggest these books to others?
- Was anything missing from these books?

Childhood

- Where and when was he born?
- Describe his parents, siblings, and friends.
- Did he grow up in unusual circumstances?

Accomplishments off the Field

- What is this person's life's work?
- Has he received awards or recognition for accomplishments?
- How have this person's accomplishments served others?

Write a Biography

Help and Obstacles

- Did this individual have a positive attitude?
- Did he receive help from others?
- Did this person have a mentor?
- Did this person face any hardships?
- If so, how were the hardships overcome?

Accomplishments on the Field

- What records does this person hold?
- What key games and plays have defined his career?
- What are his stats in categories important to his position?

Work and Preparation

- What was this person's education?
- What was his work experience?
- How does this person work?
- What is the process he uses?

Trivia Time

Take this quiz to test your knowledge of the University of Florida Gators. The answers are printed upside down under each question.

1 What are Gators fans commonly known as?

A. Gator Nation

2 How many times have the Gators won the National Championship?

A. Three

3 Who won the first Heisman Trophy for the University of Florida?

A. Steve Spurrier

4 What is the nickname for the stadium where the Gators play?

A. "The Swamp"

5 When did UF win its first National Championship?

A. 1996

6 What is the full name of the Gators' football stadium?

A. Steve Spurrier—Florida Field at Ben Hill Griffin Stadium

7 How many Heisman Trophy winners do the Gators have?

A. Three

8 What are the names of the UF team mascots?

A. Albert and Alberta

9 When did the Florida football program begin?

A. 1906

10 When was the Gators' current stadium built?

A. 1930

Key Words

drafted: chosen to play professionally in the National Football League during an annual event

Hall of Fame: a group of persons judged to be outstanding in a particular sport

iconic: famous or well-known

inducted: added as an official member of a group

logo: a symbol that stands for a team or organization

matchups: contests between two athletes or sports teams

postseason: a sporting event that takes place after the end of the regular season

Pro Bowl: the annual all-star game for NFL players pitting the best players in the National Football Conference against the best players in the American Football Conference

renovation: construction that works to improve or expand an older building

synthetic: made from chemicals that imitate a natural product

Index

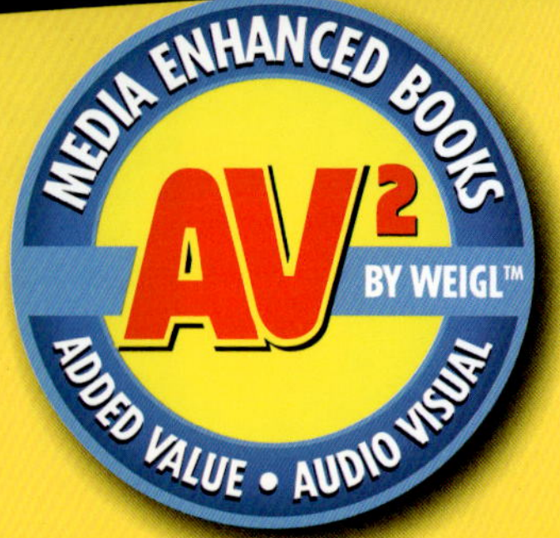

Log on to www.av2books.com

AV² by Weigl brings you media enhanced books that support active learning. Go to www.av2books.com, and enter the special code found on page 2 of this book. You will gain access to enriched and enhanced content that supplements and complements this book. Content includes video, audio, weblinks, quizzes, a slideshow, and activities.

AV² Online Navigation

Audio
Listen to sections of the book read aloud.

Book Pages
AV² pages directly correspond to pages in the book.

Video
Watch informative video clips.

Embedded Weblinks
Gain additional information for research.

Key Words
Study vocabulary, and complete a matching word activity.

Try This!
Complete activities and hands-on experiments.

Quizzes
Test your knowledge.

Slideshow
View images and captions, and prepare a presentation.

AV² was built to bridge the gap between print and digital. We encourage you to tell us what you like and what you want to see in the future.

Sign up to be an AV² Ambassador at www.av2books.com/ambassador.

Due to the dynamic nature of the internet, some of the URLs and activities provided as part of AV² by Weigl may have changed or ceased to exist. AV² by Weigl accepts no responsibility for any such changes. All media enhanced books are regularly monitored to update addresses and sites in a timely manner. Contact AV² by Weigl at 1-866-649-3445 or av2books@weigl.com with any questions, comments, or feedback.